My Little Friend®

GOES TO SCHOOL

By Evelyn M. Finnegan

Illustrations by Diane R. Houghton

LITTLE FRIEND PRESS

SCITUATE, MASSACHUSETTS

First U.S. edition 1996.
Printed in China. Published
in the United States
by Little Friend Press,
Scituate, Massachusetts.

ISBN 0-9641285-3-5

Library of Congress
Catalog Card Number: 96-075797

Second Printing

LITTLE FRIEND PRESS
28 NEW DRIFTWAY
SCITUATE, MASSACHUSETTS 02066

*To Paul and Mary many thanks
for your thoughtful and caring hearts.*

*To my grandson Alex whose loving manner
made this book all the more meaningful.*

Alex is going
to school.

His mother helps
him put on his
green sweater.

The teacher is happy
showing Alex and his
mom around the school.

MONDAY

COOL

5

There are easels for painting,
blocks for building, puzzles,
crayons and buckets of clay...

SHAPES

a fish tank, a play
house, a general store
and lots of books.

Best of all there is
a fluffy white
bunny whose name
is Marshmallow.

Next the teacher shows Alex the
bathroom for him to use if he needs to.

When it is time for Alex's
mom to leave she whispers,
"Dad and Grandmummy
will be here at twelve o'clock
to pick you up."

The children sit
on a green rug
for meeting time.

When it is Alex's
turn he shows the
children his
favorite sweater...

14

the one his nana
knit with the
secret pocket for
Little Friend.

The children like
it very much.

HANNA   AMY   ALEX   MOLLY   BRENDAN

When they finish, Alex goes
to hang up his sweater.

The cubby has his name on it.

The children sit at a round
table for their snack.

Alex passes the cookies to Sam.

During free time Alex and his new friend
Sam enjoy painting at the easels.

Everyone is busy. There is lots to do.

What do you think Alex will do next?

Then the teacher says,
"let's clean up now, it's
almost time to go home."

Alex helps put the blocks
away and then goes to
his cubby...

"Where's Little Friend?"

Everyone started
looking for
Little Friend.

The teacher checked
inside the pots
and pans.

Alex looked in
the fish tank.

George sifted
through the sand.

Amy searched on
the science table.

Alex felt sad.

Suddenly Molly shouted,
"look what's in Marshmallow's cage!"

They all laughed!

Alex got down on his tummy and looked into Marshmallow's cage.

"Bunny that's mine!
I need to bring
Little Friend home
with me. You have
your own toy."

"I'm glad you like my
Little Friend," said Alex.

"Maybe I'll let you play
with him tomorrow."